A Parents Magazine
READ ALOUD AND EASY READING PROGRAM® Original.

Library of Congress Cataloging in Publication Data
Kent, Jack 1920-   The biggest shadow in the zoo.
SUMMARY: Goober the elephant is distressed when he
loses his shadow.
[1. Elephants—Fiction.   2. Shades and shadows—
Fiction]   I. Title.
PZ7.K414Bi   [E]   80–25517
ISBN 0–8193–1047–6
ISBN 0–8193–1048–4 (lib. bdg.)

THE BIGGEST SHADOW IN THE ZOO

by JACK KENT

Parents Magazine Press
NEW YORK

To Mary Lou and Dudley

Copyright © 1981 by Jack Kent
All rights reserved
Printed in the United States of America
10 9 8 7 6 5 4 3 2

Goober was an elephant
who lived at the zoo.
Goober was very special.
At least HE thought so.

All the other animals
lived in cages or behind bars.
Goober lived on an island
with a moat all around it.
But that wasn't why
Goober thought he was special.

There was a bridge over the moat
with a sign on it.
The sign said, "Elephant Rides 10¢."
Twice a day—in the morning
and the afternoon—a box was strapped
onto Goober's back.
Children sat in the box,
and Goober gave them a ride.
The children loved Goober
and fed him peanuts.
But that wasn't why
Goober thought he was special.

ELEPHANT
RIDES
10¢

From his island, Goober could see
most of the other animals.
They were all sizes — big and
small and in between.
And they were all shapes —
fat and thin and some very strange.
Goober noticed that each animal
had a shadow. And the shadow was
big or small or fat or thin,
just like the animal.

Goober noticed something else.
HIS shadow was the BIGGEST
shadow in the zoo.
And THAT was the reason
Goober thought he was special.

Goober was very fond of his shadow.
And his shadow seemed fond of Goober.
They were always together.
They were very good friends.

One day Goober was catching peanuts
that the children were throwing to him.
His shadow was with him, as usual.
When Goober swung his trunk to catch
a peanut, his shadow swung its trunk
and pretended to catch one too.

Goober forgot to watch where he was going
and got so close to the moat that
he almost fell in. His shadow DID.

When Goober leaned over
the edge of the moat,
he could see his shadow
down on the bottom.
Goober was quite upset.
He was afraid his shadow
got hurt in the fall.

Goober stood very still
and watched his shadow
for several minutes.
It didn't move.

"It's dead!" thought Goober.
"But how could such a little fall
kill it? My shadow is tough.
I've stepped on it lots of times,
and I didn't hurt it.
I don't understand."
And he shook his head.
The shadow shook its head too.

It was all right!
Goober felt much better.
But his shadow was still
at the bottom of the moat
and Goober couldn't get it out.

Soon it was time for the
afternoon elephant ride.
Goober's trainers strapped his box
onto his back.
"Come on, Goober," they said.

But Goober didn't move.
He and his shadow had always
been together.
Goober couldn't leave it now,
when it was in trouble.

The trainers pushed and pulled.

They scolded and coaxed.

But Goober refused to budge.

So they unstrapped the box
and told the children
there wouldn't be any
elephant ride today
because Goober
wasn't feeling well.

The animal doctor came,
but he couldn't find
anything wrong with Goober.

"It's probably just something he ate,"
said the doctor.
"I'll check him again in the morning."

Night came. Goober couldn't see
his shadow anymore, but he
stayed to keep it company.
Rain started to fall.
There was a flash of lightning.
By its light, Goober could see
that his shadow was still there.
He saw something else, too.
The water in the moat was getting deeper.
Goober didn't know if his shadow could swim.
Goober worried and worried
and wished the night would end.

The rain stopped by morning,
but thick clouds hid the sun.
Goober looked over the edge of the moat.
The water was almost to the top.
And Goober's shadow was no where to be seen.

"It drowned!" thought Goober.
"I'll never see it again!"

Goober walked slowly and sadly
toward the elephant house.
He looked back, hoping to
see his shadow.
But it wasn't there.
He felt like crying.

Goober went inside
his dark house.
He wanted to be left alone,
so he tried to
hide in the corner.
"Feeling better this morning?"
said a voice.
It was the doctor.

The doctor lit a lantern
so he could see Goober.
And Goober saw something that
made his heart leap for joy.
There in the corner . . .
the very corner Goober was facing . . .
was his SHADOW! As big as ever!
Being in the water all night
hadn't even shrunk it.

Goober didn't know how long his shadow
had been in the elephant house —
or how it got there.
But it didn't matter.
They were together again, and that
was the most important thing.
"Well, well," the doctor said to Goober.
"I don't know what the trouble WAS,
but there's nothing wrong with you NOW."
He gave Goober a pat, turned off the lantern,
and went to check on the other animals.

Without the light from the lantern
Goober couldn't see his shadow any more.
But he knew it was there,
safe and sound.
Goober was very happy.

He ate
a good breakfast
and had a nice nap.
It had been
a long night.

When it was time for
the morning elephant ride,
Goober's trainers led him outside
and strapped on his box.
The clouds had gone away.
The sun was shining brightly.
Goober looked at his shadow
and smiled happily.

The children got their dimes' worth.
Goober gave them an extra long ride
because he felt so good.
But he was very, very careful
not to go anywhere near the moat.
And his shadow always stayed close by.

ABOUT THE AUTHOR

As a teenager, JACK KENT was already earning
money from his artwork. He worked in commercial
art and drew magazine cartoons until 1968, when
he published his first children's book. He has since
written and illustrated more than 40 books for children. *The Biggest Shadow in the Zoo* is Mr. Kent's
third book as author/artist for Parents' new line,
following *Socks for Supper* and *Piggy Bank
Gonzales*. He also illustrated Jane Yolen's *The
Simple Prince*.

Mr. Kent says, "Like Goober, I have noticed that my shadow is only around on nice,
sunshiny days. On rainy days, when I'd like to
have some company, my shadow is nowhere to be
found. It's probably curled up in some nice, dry
place, waiting for the rain to stop."

Mr. Kent lives with his wife, June, in San
Antonio, Texas. The city zoo has a moat around
the elephant yard, just like the one where Goober
lives. Mr. Kent thinks Goober would be very
happy in San Antonio. And so would his shadow!